WOODY AND JUNE VERSUS WINSLOW

WOODY AND JUNE VERSUS WINSLOW

WOODY AND JUNE VERSUS THE APOCALYPSE, EPISODE 10

ROBERT J. MCCARTER

LITTLE HUMMINGBIRD PUBLISHING

WOODY AND JUNE VERSUS THE APOCALYPSE

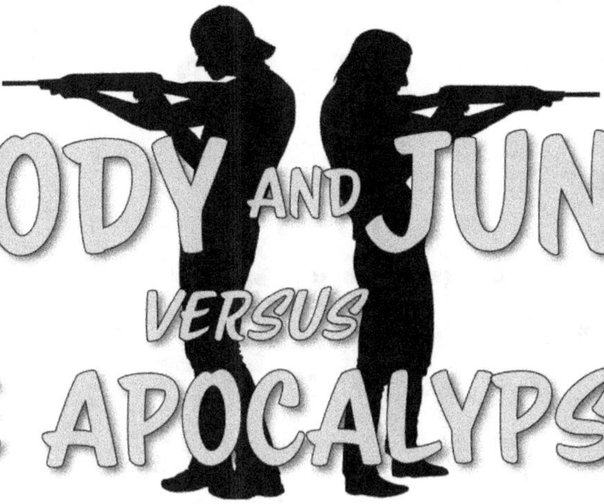

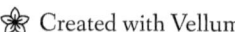

CHAPTER ONE

JUNE IS DRIVING our now well-used pickup east down I-40 towards Winslow, Arizona, and I am in the backseat fiddling with dynamite.

That's the apocalypse for you. The gorgeous girl of my dreams is feet away from me, but to rescue our friend Dallas from June's crazy ex Talia—a psychotic, petty, wannabe warlord if there ever was one —I have to work with explosives. In a speeding vehicle that is rumbling down a post-apocalyptic highway.

You would think you could go as fast as you want. No other cars, relatively flat, the high desert of Arizona stretching out in all directions. But the road is not maintained. There is debris. There are wrecks here and there. Wandering zombies who are really stupid about cars and will shamble right in front of you.

We shouldn't even be on the highway. Our plan, after escaping Talia several times, was to hightail it south and east over the dirt roads that crisscross much of the open land of Arizona to the White Mountains.

But no. I wanted a moment. I thought Arizona was big enough for us to get lost in. I underestimated Talia.

And to be fair, we were beat to shit after our first two escapes.

I've got a scabbed-over flesh wound on my forehead from when Talia almost blew my brains out and a hole in my left arm from one of her goons as we tried to escape yet again. June's face has purple going to yellow bruises from her fist fight with Talia. We really needed a moment.

And to be even more fair, once we had that moment, once we were poised for escape, we realized what kind of damage Talia and her new gang would do to some decent people living in a good situation at Phantom Ranch down at the bottom of the Grand Canyon. It's hot down there, but it is isolated and there is an endless supply of water from the Colorado River making it a pretty perfect place to wait out the apocalypse. So we changed our plan. We turned back and headed back towards the Grand Canyon.

But we had given her enough time and Talia was ready for us. This is round two of Talia's "game." Her stated rules are:

1. *I win.*
2. *The more you play, the longer you survive.*
3. *I win.*

June and I survived Two Guns and the Apache Death Cave, where Talia attempted to recreate what the Apache experienced there in 1878 with a little zombie booby trap thrown in for good measure. But she captured Dallas. Left us a clue. Gave us a deadline.

Thus June driving as fast as is sort of safe while I play with dynamite in the backseat of the Toyota pickup truck that was new when the apocalypse happened, but has seen a hell of a lot of action in the few weeks since I liberated it from the car dealership in Flagstaff.

Its beautiful black paint is dusty and scratched and there are bullet holes in the tailgate. The rear window has been removed, something we did after being chased across those high desert dirt roads with people shooting at us, so we can move freely from the bed into the truck.

It's morning and the air is still cool, the windows down as the chaotic wind rushes through.

"I love you, June Medina," I say as I insert a blasting cap into a stick of dynamite. These things need to be said. Especially now. Especially today. Especially while messing with dynamite.

"I love you, Woody Beckman," she says back, her voice cheerful.

This is only day twenty-seven of Woody and June versus the Apocalypse, but my feelings for her are deep.

June is ex-army, tough as hell, but petite, athletic, and pixie-beautiful with her short black hair, olive skin, and ocean-blue eyes. She's smart. She's a survivor. And despite a devastating apocalypse, we found each other.

I chuckle. Her cheerfulness gives me hope. We are speeding to face the one thing in this world that June Medina is afraid of. Her crazy ex Talia. And isn't that ironic? Even post-apocalypse, everyone's got a crazy ex.

"What are you laughing about?" she asks.

I shrug. "I'm with the girl of my dreams and she's driving the truck I always wanted and I am playing with dynamite. What more can a boy ask for?"

"Brace," she says sharply. And I do, holding the old stick of dynamite close, right before the truck swerves to the left, off the pavement onto the wide median, as we avoid a three-car-pileup, and back onto the road.

In a flash, I see a Z banging on the window of one of the crumpled cars. It is mummy-like, having been trapped in there for over a year. A couple more years and I figure it will "die." Zombies need sustenance to survive. It's not quite like the shows I used to watch.

"So you think we've got a chance?" she asks, her voice tentative.

"I think Talia wants Dallas and me dead," I say. "I think she wants you back. I think this stupid game of hers is supposed to accomplish both of those things."

I could say more. That these elaborate and dangerous traps and games are ridiculous. That Talia is psychotic. That the apocalypse broke her, badly. But I don't. June served in Afghanistan with Talia and was once in love with her. Before the world went to hell. Before Talia broke.

"And our chances...?" she says.

I wrap the finished piece of dynamite complete with fuse and blasting cap into an old rag and carefully set it down. I lean forward so my face is closer to June's. As the wind whips around us, I can smell the dry desert and her sweat, a whiff of smoke clinging to her clothes from our escape of the Apache Death Cave. But there's still something sweet about the way she smells. Despite the infrequent bathing and the crazy few days we've had, there is something decidedly June about her scent, and I can't get enough of it.

"Phantom Company ended up turning against her because of all the energy she was expending to catch you," I say.

She bites her lips and nods. "Yeah..."

"Well, she just took over this Flagstaff tribe of survivors and look at how much more energy she is expending trying to capture you."

I see her blue eyes widen in the rearview mirror. "So...," she says, "we are going to try to survive long enough so that they turn on her too?"

I nod and lean back. "And they will. She just took over. They don't really know her. They certainly don't trust her. They are doing everything they are doing right now because they are terrified of her. That can't last."

June catches my eye in the rearview mirror. "I hope you are right."

I hope I am too.

CHAPTER TWO

FROM THE GHOST town of Twin Arrows to the outskirts of Winslow, Arizona is a bit over twenty miles. June drives and I prepare as fast as I can.

Backpacks. Dynamite. Managing the little solar chargers we have on top of things in the back of the truck and swapping in charged batteries to our flashlights and other electronic gear.

Since Talia found us in the off-the grid plots of land called the 40s northeast of Flagstaff, we haven't prepared properly. And almost more than those stops we made, that lack of prep was a mistake.

When I was on my own, I would have never made this kind of mistake. I let myself relax too much. I let myself think that with June and Dallas everything would be fine.

But it's not.

"Get off here," I say from the backseat. We are at the I-40 business exit for Winslow. The town has a whopping three exits off the I-40 with a total population of less than ten thousand before the Zs came.

The land is fairly flat here, more of the high desert we've been driving through with red-tinged earth and lots of grass and weeds starting to green up. To the north of the highway is a cluster of low homes with trees big enough to make it look like an older neighborhood. To the south of the highway is the historic downtown that features the corner the Eagles sang about in "Take it Easy." Our clue in this game Talia is having us play.

"Take it easy now," I say with a grin as June pulls onto the off-ramp and around an abandoned car.

"You're a real comedian," she says with only a small grin. "Maybe you should take that routine on the road."

Survival. Laughter. And June. Those are my rules for each post-apocalypse day. Laughter, the real kind, is hard to come by so I've got to make my chances.

"The Woody and June comedy extravaganza with guest star Dallas," I say, lowering my voice so it kind of sounds like a radio guy from the fifties. "Featuring bad puns, lame jokes, and the not-to-be missed zombie fun run where Woody, June, and Dallas try to make a zombie laugh and not get eaten."

She flashes me a tight-lipped smile and I get the message. Not the time. Or not funny enough for the situation.

I look at my watch. "We've got sixteen minutes to find her." That is what is left of the hour Talia gave us. Her time limits are to make us rush, keep us from thinking.

It's a long, easy off-ramp and the town has that post-apocalyptic abandoned look. Debris on the street. Abandoned and crashed cars in the road. Buildings looking unkempt with peeling paint.

Some of this is not a new look for Winslow. The little town struggled after the highway came and routed most of the traffic around Winslow. The last time I was here, before it all happened, there were plenty of abandoned buildings that already had a post-apocalyptic vibe.

"Right and then left," I tell June at the end of the off-ramp. It's just a short jog between two gas stations and then left onto Old Route 66.

There's a nice sign to greet us. A round slab of stone with red writing that says, "Welcome to Winslow." The stone is nestled in layers of sandstone making you think of the Grand Canyon. It's a little cheesy but it's also kind of nice.

The road is divided, two lanes in both directions. Nice lampposts in the middle. Winslow was making a go of it, tourism-wise, and it was all centered around that Eagles song.

I stop with the terrible attempts at comedy and watch. This section of the road is kind of industrial. Mini-storage, garages, low buildings without signs, an old Roadway Inn. Definitely not historic in the normal sense. Around this part of the country "historic" are things built when the area was first settled, back in the late 1800s.

June takes it easy, easing us around wrecks and keeping the pace steady.

There are no Zs and it's as eerie as hell because of it. This is proof of what Dallas told us, that when Talia's group came this way they lured and trapped the Zs so they could scrounge through town at their leisure. I mean, at least without any free-roaming Zs. I'm sure there are plenty trapped in buildings.

Talia used her new recruits as bait for the Zs and Dallas was a new recruit when she came through with them. All of this makes my stomach twist worrying about what Talia did to Dallas.

The road is in really good shape, it must have been resurfaced not long before it all went to hell. The sidewalks are also in good shape with young deciduous trees just leafed out for spring along with those nice streetlights sprouting out of the narrow median.

The road flows to the south a bit and then straightens out and runs parallel to the railroad tracks, some tanker cars visible.

Older homes appear on the left as the two sides of Route 66 split.

"Stay to the right," I say.

We pass the remnants of a convenience store and a bunch of bland homes that look like they were built in the sixties. The houses are small, single story, with more carports than garages. The yards are mostly dirt with some sad, struggling grass, but they probably looked that way before the apocalypse. It's hard to grow grass in the desert.

We pass some low apartments. Some bigger nondescript buildings. A billboard for a trading post. A laundromat that looks like it used to be a house. A sprawling two-story motel.

Except for the debris on the road, the cars parked awkwardly, and the lack of the living, this is kind of what it was like to drive through this part of Winslow. A sleepy old town that looks like it had seen better days.

Except now all towns look like they have seen better days.

The "historic" part is only a few blocks where the houses get nicer, where a simple church made out of red sandstone rises up, where a few buildings from the late 1800s sit right on the sidewalk built of red bricks.

It's about two miles from the off-ramp to the corner the Eagles sang about, the corner of Route 66 and Kinsley Avenue. You can't miss it. The pavement has been replaced with brick pavers and a huge black and white "Arizona US 66" is painted in the middle of it, the top pointing to the north. It's the exact same shape as a highway route sign with a rounded and pointed bottom and a scalloped top.

We get there without incident. Every wreck we pass, every empty building, every broken-out window making us more nervous. Something should be happening. Zs should be swarming. Talia's people should be attacking.

There's no mistaking it when we get there. Besides the enormous Route 66 sign painted on the brick, there are two life-sized bronze statues of Glenn Frey there. One with short hair and an acoustic guitar resting on his boot standing next to an old-fashioned street-lamp that has a sign that says "Standin' on the Corner" in case you had any doubt.

One lamppost up Kinsley Avenue is a younger version of Frey with long hair, his outstretched hand leaning against the lamppost. I don't remember that one—I think it must be newer.

Behind all of this is a façade, a single wall built up to look like a historic building complete with fake windows. The windows are murals that show some kind of a furniture store and the reflection of a blonde in an old red Ford pickup slowing down to look at Frey.

And Dallas is there. Handcuffed and chained to the first statue, still in her pink down coat. She is standing behind him, her back to the "Standin' on the Corner" lamppost, her cuffed hands are around his neck and a chain looping around her handcuffs and through the gap between the guitar and the statue's leg. She's not going anywhere.

"About time," she calls when we get close. She nods at the statue. "I mean, I know that I've been desperate for some company, but this dude is made of bronze and not much of a talker for being a famous songwriter and all."

The street, like the rest of the town, is quiet. Too damn quiet. The challenge here can't be to free Dallas. And it seems like that wasn't part of the original plan anyway but was forced by Dallas's refusal to go into the Apache Death Cave.

June drives the Toyota up onto the curb.

"You okay?" she asks.

Dallas shrugs, the gesture strange in her faux fur edged puffy pink jacket. "They didn't hurt me, and the little weeny bitch didn't show her face, but the handcuff key holes are filled with epoxy or something like that so no getting them off the easy way. This sure as hell has got to be a trap."

By "little weeny bitch" Dallas meant Talia. That was kind of like her psycho pet name for her.

I get out and look at my watch. "Three minutes." I walk over to Dallas. She's got ankle cuffs on too. I crouch down and rub at the dark block over the keyhole. It's hard and smooth. June has a collection of handcuff keys—no idea why—but they are not going to help.

"So get me out of this, okay, Woody?" Dallas says, a pleading smile on her round face.

I just stand there looking at her. And then looking around. I spot a drone up high descending rapidly, the buzz of its four propellers just becoming audible.

No people. No zombies. Just over three minutes. It can't be as easy as hacksawing her loose. And then it hits me. What Dallas told me about them luring the zombie hordes and containing them.

"Move the truck so the back of it is facing Dallas," I say, my tone urgent, my words quick. "Now!"

CHAPTER THREE

"WHAT'S GOING ON, WOODY?" June asks, her blue eyes darting around the quiet corner of Winslow looking for danger.

"Get me the hell out of here," Dallas says.

I open my mouth to tell them what I fear is about to happen when two other things happen. The drone does a close flyby and the walkie talkie, still in the truck, squawks to life.

"Hey there, kiddies," Talia says. "Thanks for playing. Your prize, should you choose to accept it, is to make a choice. Woody and June, you can live to fight another day, or you can all die trying to save Dallas."

There is a brief moment of silence.

"Oh, and I've added one more rule to our fun little game," she continues with a chuckle. "You shoot, we shoot. So leave the firearms out of this next little chapter."

I look around, up high. The façade is about twenty feet tall, they could have someone there, or better yet the historic brick building across the street, the one that houses the "Standin' On The Corner" shop that contains everything you could imagine in terms of Eagles and Winslow merchandise. It's taller with a great view of the area.

Catty-corner to it is another gift shop, a lower building, but they could have someone up there too.

I go back to the car and grab the walkie. I need more information. "So we shoot, you shoot yourself, Talia?" I ask. "Is that what you are saying?"

"No, Mr. Woodpecker," she says. "You shoot anything, and we shoot Dallas."

I look at Dallas and she's gone white, as white as the trim of her pink coat once was. It's now clear that Talia means for her to die today.

"Thirty seconds until the fun starts, kiddies," Talia says on the walkie. "Best get your boy toy and start driving, June-bug."

The walkie goes dead for a few seconds and then it starts playing music. Oddly, it takes me a moment to recognize it. It's the same song that was played on this corner nonstop since they turned it into a tourist destination. The same song in which Glenn Frey wrote about this corner.

"Take it Easy" plays over the walkie talkie and for some reason the song strikes terror in my heart.

I DON'T LIKE to be right. Not when it comes to my fears. I like it best when they are something that wake me up in the middle of the night, keeps me awake for a few hours, and then I feel silly about it in the morning when my fears prove to be overblown. It was just my imagination, nothing real. Back before the Zs, the imagination was often worse than reality. For a middle-class white American living in Arizona, my imagination was usually worse than the reality.

But post-apocalypse? Not so much.

I spin around. This is historic downtown Winslow. Older brick buildings. Nice wide sidewalks. Trees, metal park benches, and ornate streetlamps.

It should be filled with tourists, people smiling at the happy song, taking selfies with the statues of Frey, posing in front of the mural with that girl slowing down.

But it's empty. The roads covered in dirt and leaves and a little garbage. An old wreck between two cars south of us down Kinsley Avenue.

And then I think I am just being silly. Talia isn't going to do it, she's not really going to unleash all those caged zombies with the only living people here June, Dallas, and I and the shooter up on one of these buildings.

Zombies that old, that hungry, that many of them, would sense us instantly with their fresh-brains fungus network radar. They would come for us. And their hunger might make them a little weak, but their numbers and their desperation would more than make up for that.

"What," Dallas says. "What do you see?" She's swiveling her head around, the chain rattling against bronze, looking down the streets.

June has moved the truck so the back end is up on the curb, about six feet from Dallas. She's looking around too.

"No..." June whispers. "She wouldn't."

"Wouldn't what?" Dallas asks. She's starting to panic, pulling on her restraints, her face flushing with the effort.

"Let the Zs go," June says quietly.

Dallas goes still, her mouth dropping open, her face paling again. She gives a sharp little nod, bites her lip, and then expels a stream of wicked curses aimed at Talia.

"Oh she will," she says when she gets herself under control. "That's what this damn thing is, putting me out for a bunch of Zs to eat. You..." She falters and then her brown eyes find mine. "Don't let me die that way, Woody. Don't let me become one of them."

I take a step back. The song is still playing through the walkie, urging us to "Take it easy." To not let things make us crazy. Normally an ethic I'm all about, but I just want to break the damn walkie-talkie.

I know exactly what Dallas is asking me to do. Dallas wants me to shoot her. In the head. It's the only way to make sure she doesn't become a Z.

I feel dizzy. This is too much. This is what Talia wants. She wants us to murder our own friend.

I stumble over to the truck, open one of the tubs, and pull a hacksaw out.

"No," I say. It comes out loud, but I can hear the fear in my voice. The chain between the cuffs is under the statue's chin. There isn't even a place for me to get the saw in. What we need is bolt cutters, but we don't have them.

"Can you get your hands up over his head?" I ask.

"Promise me, Woody," she hisses at me. "Promise me."

We are close and her breath is a bit dank. Not enough brushing of teeth or drinking of water, or eating of food for that matter.

A wave of dizziness hits me again and I can still smell the smoke and taste it from the Apache Death Cave. I cough as if the memory of the smoke is almost as bad as the real thing. I prepared on the way over here, but I didn't eat anything and only had a few sips of water.

I prepared gear but not myself.

"Can you get your hands over his head?" I ask. "I can't get the saw in."

June is out of the truck in the middle of the street, on the big white and black "Arizona US 66" sign. She's slowly turning, watching all four roads.

"Promise me, Woody," Dallas says, and her voice breaks. "No zombie Dallas. Promise me!" She's breathing heavy as if she were running from zombies.

I look into her brown eyes, they are filling with tears, full of desperation. She doesn't think she's going to get out of this and is making her last wish. And that wish is for me to kill her and destroy her brain so she just dies and the fungus doesn't get her and turn her into a Z.

It's a moment. I smell Dallas's breath. Hear my heartbeat. My mouth tastes like ash. My stomach is roiling. My hands are shaking.

Dallas who appeared at first to be an enemy and then became the truest of friends. Dallas who went on an ill-prepared and insane rafting trip down the Colorado River through the Grand Canyon with me. Dallas who went to war with me to get June back from Talia and Phantom Ranch at the bottom of the Grand Canyon. Dallas who is my best friend in this insane post-apocalyptic world.

"I promise," I whisper. "But we're going to get out of this. All of us."

I don't know if I believe it, but Dallas nods, leans closer to the statue so she has some slack, and pulls her hands up. But her hands stop at his forehead. There is another longer chain, looped around the cuffs and down under the right hand of the statue, through the gap between the guitar and his leg. She can't get her hands over his head.

I drop the saw and push on her cuffs. Hard. The cuffs cut into Dallas's wrist. She grunts in pain, but it doesn't work. There isn't enough length in the chain.

I follow the chain down and it is joined with a padlock and we don't have the key.

That left me trying to hacksaw through the thick chain instead of the small chain joining the handcuffs. That would take hours.

"Remember your promise," Dallas says.

I ignore her and look around as if a bolt cutter might magically appear. The drone is hovering right over June in the middle of the street. The truck is full of useful gear, but nothing for this. And then I remember the hand ax.

"What is it?" Dallas asks. She must have seen the thought cross my face.

"Your hand," I say with a grim nod and make a chopping motion.

"Oh no," she says. "Oh, hell no."

And I don't blame her. Forget the pain, try surviving with one hand. Or even surviving the wound and the blood loss and the probable infection.

I keep looking around, hoping for some kind of inspiration. Some kind of way out of this.

But there's nothing. The music keeps playing, all tinny and scratchy from the walkie-talkie, the drone keeps hovering, and the tourist trap has turned into a literal trap for the three of us.

"Here they come," June says, pointing down Route 66 back the way we came. "Jesus Christ," she whispers. "There are so many."

CHAPTER FOUR

THE STATUE of Glenn Frey is bolted to the cement. Dallas is handcuffed and chained to the statue. And the Zs are coming.

"Thousands of them," June calls from the center of the street. "Holy shit! There are thousands of them."

"Take it Easy" is playing over the walkie-talkie, the drone is buzzing above us, and there is a gunman somewhere ready to shoot Dallas if we use our guns.

"Do it!" Dallas says, her voice fierce but her pale face showing terror. "Do it, Woody, and get out of here."

I ignore her. "How long?" I yell to June.

She shrugs. "Two minutes. Maybe less."

I nod like that's good news or something.

"Do it, Woody!" Dallas yells.

"I need you, June," I say as I start throwing open tubs in the back of the truck.

June runs up, her ocean-blue eyes fierce and focused. "What's the plan?"

I nod to the statue and Dallas. "We're taking both of them with us. But I need you to rig it up. I'm going to go slow the Zs down."

Her forehead scrunches as she wonders what I can do against

thousands of zombies and then she remembers what I was doing on the way over here and nods.

I pull out a thick tow rope and a couple of ratchet straps. I dive under the truck and loop one end around the frame of the truck, and then go to the statue.

I can hear them now. The zombies. The thousands of collective growls and snarls and shuffling turning into this tsunami of white nose. This terrifying wave of sound. And I can start to smell the stench of them, the rotting meat fungus funk is flowing out in front of them.

I take the other end of the strap and stare at the statue. I want to loop it around the neck, it needs to be up high, but Dallas's hands are there.

"Go!" June says, taking the tow rope from me. "I got this."

"What the hell is happening?" Dallas asks as I run back to the truck.

"We are taking you and your boyfriend with us," June says, with more than a little amusement in her voice.

I grab the backpack that I prepared from the backseat. "Use the ratchet straps to pull the statue's head off the ground after you pull it down. And use low gears and four-wheel-drive," I shout as I run past them to the west.

"I know how to drive," June calls after me. "Have fun with your friends, darling."

I almost look back. I want to see those blue eyes again and that beautiful face. I want to understand what the hell has gotten into her. She was all business when we drove in, when the streets were deserted, and we didn't know what the danger would be. And now that we have thousands of Zs bearing down on us and a shitty chance of getting away with Dallas, she's being all cheerful and light.

Maybe she's faking it. Maybe it's the not knowing that gets to her and now that she knows what we are up against she feels better. Whatever it is, I hope we all live long enough so I can find out.

And then I see the Zs and nearly shit myself. We faced the tourist zombie horde on the rim of the Grand Canyon, maybe five hundred strong. But this. This is something else. It's like a parade of Zs coming down the street. No, streets. It seems that they were all trapped to the west of us and are coming in from multiple directions, a shambling horde of hunger and only the three of us to eat.

I put the backpack on, but facing front. It looks dorky, it feels weird, but I need access to what's in it. And what's in it is dynamite. All prepared with blasting caps and fuses.

I shove my bat between the backpack and my chest. It's awkward as hell, but I might need it. Talia says if we shoot, they shoot Dallas, so no "firearms" as she requested. Fortunately, dynamite is not a firearm.

As I stand there trying to make a plan, trying not to soil my pants, I hear Dallas says to June, "What the hell are you doing?"

"Pulling this statue down and dragging you and your boy-toy away from here," June says, her voice still cheerful. "It's the only way."

"You might kill me," Dallas says.

"And you just asked Woody to kill you," June says. "What the hell do we have to lose?"

And then their voices are drowned in the sound of the approaching horde. My wounds are forgotten in the adrenaline of it all and I run down Route 66 with the backpack bouncing in front of me, the stench getting worse, the wave of snarling, shuffling, snapping noises becoming louder.

Behind me I hear the truck start up and I say a prayer to a god I don't believe in that June can pull that statue down without killing or maiming Dallas.

As I get closer, the mass of undead starts to differentiate into individuals. Zombie soccer moms and zombie kids. Zombie construction workers and zombie tourists. All of them fairly desiccated and halfway to being mummies. All of them starving to death. All of them wanting to eat every single ounce of me.

The ones out front have good legs, although some have broken arms, some have half-ripped-off faces, all with dirty and torn clothing, the whites of their eyes gone yellow.

And those shows you watched where Zs could live forever on nothing but air? That's not the way it works. I am convinced, although I have not been able to test this yet, that a Z has a limited lifespan if it doesn't find something to eat.

Think about it. Sure, they have fungus brains and a network of fungus permeating their bodies—we proved that at the South Rim of the Grand Canyon—but they expend energy. That has to come from somewhere. And the Z can only consume its own body for so long. They eat to live, just like we do.

Well... not just like we do. I'm not a psycho undead cannibal. And how they absorb energy must be different because I've never seen zombie poop. And I really don't want to see zombie poop. But they eat and absorb energy from what they eat. The fungus network that takes over the bodies somehow processing the food and distributing the energy.

This bunch of Zs bearing down on me has been locked up for six months or so, without a thing to eat. That makes them weak but very, very desperate.

But none of that really matters. It's the number of them that counts. If we were facing off with this many angry and determined kittens we'd be screwed.

I get close enough so the sound of them is all I can hear, and the stench is making me gag. While there is still the rotting meat smell, it's a bit less than with a fresher zombie, but that is more than made up for by the putrid fungal bouquet. It's so bad I can taste it, like I'm eating handfuls of mold.

I shake it off and focus on what I am doing. I prepared three different length fuses. Thirty seconds. Twenty seconds. And ten seconds.

I take one of each out, stick two in the webbing on the front of the backpack, and pull out my Bic lighter from the pocket of my jeans. I found it somewhere along the way after I escaped Phoenix and before I met June. It used to be red, but the plastic cylinder is worn down and speckled with white. I light a stick with a thirty-second fuse.

They are about twenty feet away and I am just about to piss myself being this close to this many. I chuck the stick of dynamite back into the horde. I was never a pitcher, but my arm is way better than someone who never played baseball. I've got power still and decent accuracy.

I do the same with the twenty-second and ten-second sticks, throwing them all back about the same distance and distributing them across the road.

And then I run. For about five seconds. And then they explode. Not all together. I'm not that good, but it's a boom... boom... boom.

And now we pause for a brief lesson on dynamite. This isn't the movies, and while one stick of dynamite can do some damage—it can split up and move about a ton of rock—it is not nearly as powerful in the open where the expanding gasses have room to travel.

It's not like a grenade, there is no shrapnel, just a powerful concussive blast.

These are the old sticks of dynamite I got from the construction site at Padre Canyon east of Flagstaff, old sticks of dynamite with some of the nitroglycerin crystalizing and oozing out. Now, I only took the safest sticks, but running with a backpack full of old dynamite isn't exactly safe.

These particular sticks of dynamite are pretty high in nitroglycerin, so maybe they could move more than a ton of rock, but we're not talking fireballs or anything like that.

Okay, so end of lesson.

I'm running from the parade of zombies. I hear the boom... boom... boom of the dynamite going off, the sound of it making my ears ring. I feel a blast of hot air, not enough to throw me to the ground or anything, and then it starts raining. Zombie parts.

The blast may not have been contained, but I threw it into the thick of the horde and it did its job ripping through flesh.

A severed foot lands in front of me and then something hits me on the back of the head. Speaking of heads, a couple splat on the pavement near me and crack open revealing the cauliflower-like thing that has replaced most of the grey matter.

I gag at the stench of it and crouch down as body parts rain down on me, slamming into my back, splatting sickeningly against the pavement.

It doesn't last long and I turn and look.

There are holes in the horde. The places where each stick of dynamite exploded cleared about a six-foot radius. Beyond that, it still did damage, knocking Zs down. And beyond that it did... nothing. The front part of the horde is undaunted and still wants my brains and every other part of me.

Some of the zombies that were knocked down are getting up. They don't care for their fellow Zs and they don't feel the loss, they just feel their hunger, and I can hear their collective snarl through the ringing in my ears.

I run forward a little bit, pulling three more sticks out. I can just see the truck and a little bit of the tow rope, taut behind it, straining to pull the statue down.

I do the three-stick routine again, but I throw the first one so it's in front of the Zs just a bit, and then place the other two along the same lines and run.

Boom.... boom... boom...

It's raining zombies again, and I crouch down as the body parts slam into my back and legs.

I turn to look and smile. The front line of the horde has been decimated, zombie goo splattered all over the street and onto the buildings, feet and heads and arms all over the place.

But the rest of the horde is undaunted. The dynamite has ripped through about a hundred zombies and it's like it just doesn't matter. Like they will never stop coming, the susurration of their snarls and snapping jaws washing over me.

My heart flutters in my chest and my stomach clenches up.

I don't have enough dynamite and we don't have enough time.

"Woody!" June yells.

I turn and she's out of the truck and pointing toward the north emphatically.

"More Zs!" she yells. "You've got to do something."

CHAPTER FIVE

THIS IS IT. This is the moment Talia wanted us all to experience. I am running away from the zombie horde marching down Old Route 66. June is climbing back into the truck to try to pull the bronze statue of Glenn Fry down while "Take it Easy" plays all tinny on the walkie-talkie courtesy of Talia. Dallas is handcuffed and chained to the statue in her "new" pink jacket with the frilly white trim thinking this is the way she's going to die.

This is the conflict she wanted to create for us. The easy thing, the smart thing, would be for June and I to get in that truck and drive away. To leave Dallas. To survive.

And it may come down to that, but that wouldn't be the right thing to do.

I've done the wrong thing before to save my own hide in this post-apocalyptic world and it has haunted me ever since. Something that happened in the Phoenix tribe I was a part of. Maybe I'll be able to write about it someday, but not today.

I run as fast as I can. I'm a sprinter, baseball taught me how to run fast for short distances, so I run fast, pulling my baseball bat from between the backpack and my chest so I can really run, the stupid forward-facing dynamite-containing backpack bouncing up and down uncomfortably.

I toss the bat into the bed of the truck. I took it because it's a part of my identity, both pre- and post-apocalypse, but it's just in the way right now. What is a baseball back against thousands of Zs?

"Do it!" I yell to June as I run past. "Get that statue down!"

And then I see them and I want to stop and turn and run away. Anywhere. Up Kinsley Avenue towards the northeast, another parade of Zs is marching towards us. Not as many as on Route 66, but hundreds and hundreds of them.

I need June with her rifle taking them out. But that's not part of Talia's "game." We shoot, they shoot Dallas. But she didn't think to prohibit dynamite.

The Zs are spread out between the façade to my left that has the mural with the blonde and the historic red brick building to my right. They are half a block away and closer than the other marching horde with only a few trees and a couple of cars between us.

I keep running, pulling out three sticks of dynamite. I light, throw, run, and when the boom... boom... boom happens, I crouch down while it rains zombie parts.

I look back and it's not going to be enough.

I pull my last hope out of the backpack. Well, one of my last hopes. It's six sticks of dynamite duct-taped together with a single thirty-second fuse.

So, six sticks can move six tons of rock. How many Zs can it blow apart?

Through the ringing in my ears and over the noise of the Zs, I can hear the truck revving and the wheels squealing, Dallas shouting, and the sickening screech of tearing metal.

I don't turn. God, I so want to, but dynamite deserves one's singular focus. I light the bundle with my Bic, pitch it back about six feet behind the front line of Zs, and run.

This time it's a BOOM! and I feel it hit my body and I stumble forward as it rains zombie body parts around me. But I don't stop this time. There's the zombie parade on Route 66.

The statue of Glenn Fry is tilted forward, it is bending towards the bottom. June ended up wrapping the tow rope around the neck of the statue, right where Dallas is handcuffed. And this is tricky stuff. Pull the statue down too fast and you might kill Dallas. If the tow rope slips over his head, well that would rip through Dallas's arms. Don't get the statue down and the Zs get Dallas.

Almost makes me glad I'm the one fighting thousands of zombies.

The Route 66 horde is close. Too close. Only a couple of hundred feet away from Dallas. I pull out my second, and last, six-stick bundle, light it up, and throw.

I turn and run back, my breath coming fast, my mouth sour and I can taste the moldy Zs' aroma it's so thick.

I hear the BOOM! and then a wave of hot air smashes into me, but since I kept running, most of the raining down of zombie parts are behind me.

This time as I run, I notice two things. The drone is still watching and I see a head poking up above the roof of the historic building. That's the shooter, the "you shoot, we shoot" shooter. Talia wasn't bluffing about that. But there's nothing I can do about it.

As I round the corner, the truck strains forward, the metal screeches, Dallas screams, and the statue tumbles over.

I notice a couple of other things I didn't notice before. The tow rope is wrapped around the statue's neck several times, greatly reducing the chances of it slipping over his head. Dallas has work gloves on her cuffed hands and a sleeping bag shoved between her and the statue. Smart. But being chained to a bronze statue that has been just ripped from its moorings and falls to the ground is no gentle ride.

Dallas looks quite vulnerable lying on top of the statue unable to defend herself from Zs or anything else.

"Straps!" I yell as I run by. "Get the statue's head up. Now!"

My lungs are burning and it's everything I can do to keep from coughing after this morning's smoke inhalation. In fact, my voice is rough, like I've been smoking for decades and I just can't seem to get enough oxygen.

Sure, Winslow is at almost five thousand feet in elevation, quite a bit higher than Phoenix, but that doesn't explain it. It's my smoked-out lungs slowing me down.

The Kinsley Avenue Zs are even closer to June and Dallas, maybe a hundred feet away. I don't have any multi-stick bundles left, but I have about ten sticks of dynamite still in the backpack.

I look back and June has the truck close to the statue and Dallas and is rigging up the ratchet strap. I do the math in my head, thinking about the progress of the Route 66 horde and...

I don't have enough time to think it through. I only have my gut to rely on. I pull one stick out of the pack, zip it closed, shove the stick into the webbing on the back of the pack, light it and toss the whole backpack into the horde.

So this is not quite a movie-quality explosion, but it sure is something. I'm running back when the BOOOM! hits me and I go down, my ears ringing loud enough so for a moment I can't hear the damn zombies.

And then it's really raining Zs. Feet, hands, heads, and unidentifiable body parts slam into me and the street around me. An eye splats right next to me and it's like the damn Z is still staring at me, wondering how it can eat me. I can hardly hear and my stomach is rebelling at the stench of it.

I get up, I run to the back of the truck and grab my bat. There's more dynamite in there, but none of it ready. June is struggling with the ratchet strap—the statue may be too heavy for it. They need more time.

Body parts made it this far and I have to be careful of my footing. I round the corner and face off against the Route 66 zombie horde with only my baseball bat.

CHAPTER SIX

"TAKE IT EASY" is a song about a guy who feels the weight of the world on his shoulders, who's in a small town in Arizona and is looking for escape, who finds that escape when a woman in a truck that slows down to check him out.

Pure escapist fantasy. Light and fun. Catchy and happy.

Well, as I ran around that Winslow, Arizona corner, as the song continues to play on the walkie-talkie in the truck, I feel like I've got the weight of the world on my shoulders and I want to escape. Literally. I'm faced with a horde of zombies. Too many to shoot, too many to explode, and way too many to take on with just a baseball bat.

But what am I going to do? Let the Zs get to Dallas and June without a fight? Grab June, throw her in the truck, and drive away either leaving Dallas behind or dragging her with a several-hundred-pound statue?

Or fight.

Look, I'm not trying to die here. I know I can't take them all on, but maybe I can distract them, maybe I can slow them down.

The day started out with zombies and smoke inhalation and I've just been proximal to a number of blasts of dynamite and now I've been running my ass off trying to beat back two hordes of zombies. It could be I wasn't quite in my right mind. It could explain a bit of some of the choices I make.

The line of Zs is more ragged now. The blasts have done a lot of damage, causing some to fall behind. I run over to the tourist shop on the opposite side of the street of June and Dallas and down along the sidewalk until I'm only a couple of feet in front of the Zs.

"Hey, dummies!" I yell, my voice sounding hollow in my head, my ears still ringing from the blasts. Zombies can hear. It's not their prime sense, I think that fresh flesh radar is, but they can hear, so why not yell at them?

It has to be an odd sight, me with my Diamondback baseball cap and army surplus jacket taunting a horde of zombies numbered in the thousands. And I'm aware that it's odd, that it's strange on so many levels. About a year ago, I was a waiter and going to school, trying to get my life together, and now this? But I feel strangely detached. I think my brain is protecting me from the enormity of taking on a few thousands Zs with just a baseball bat.

Those zombies that are close take notice first and shamble towards me, but those behind wake up to my presence too, like the fungus group mind is feeding them new information. The horde perceptibly shifts towards me.

I want to engage. I want to take some of this manic energy and smash a few heads, but if I get close enough for that, they'll be on me.

This building is brick, painted over with tan paint and red highlights. If I could get above their reach that might distract them.

I glance over at June and Dallas and the statue is right behind the back of the truck, but it's still on the ground along with Dallas. I can see up Kinsley Avenue and that horde is getting closer. There is not much time and I can't distract both of them at once.

And I can't even distract this one effectively. The group is too long. The front of the horde has locked on to me, but I can see that as they extend down the street they are shifting towards the north side of the street, closer to where June and Dallas are.

I run back to the truck. June has the ratchet strap wrapped

around the neck of the statue like she did the tow rope, the strap coming between the statue's head and Dallas's and attached to the bumper.

The strap is tight, but not lifting the statue. It's too heavy.

"Get in the truck," I say to June. "We are out of time."

The drone is hovering low over us, but I ignore it. The Zs are seconds away, but I ignore them too. June locks her ocean-blue gaze on me and the question is there.

Can we do this to Dallas, drag her behind the truck like this? Can we cut the strap and leave her behind to save our own lives? Do I have a plan that might help?

The answer to all of those is no. We can't drag her like this. We can't leave her behind. And I have no plan. But we can't just stand here and get eaten either.

The drone is low because this is the moment Talia was waiting for. The hard choice that results in either all of us dying or Dallas being sacrificed.

The look doesn't last long, less than a second, but June purses her lips and turns towards the truck. "Go slow," I say.

MOMENTS LIKE THIS ARE BAD. Heart beating hard, adrenaline flowing, sweat beading, brain racing bad.

There is nothing in the world but our problem. Dallas cuffed to the statue, the Zs bearing down, June putting the truck in gear and gently easing it forward.

I get down low and look. There is room for her hands in the gap between the neck and the face of the statue. That's good.

I stow my bat in the back end of the truck and start trying the ratchet. It's a small ratchet, and when you are using these as tie-downs they don't have hundreds of pounds of weight on them. There's not much leverage.

"Pull your hands up," I say as the truck starts to inch forward and the statue screeches against the broad pavers with people's names on them. It's a small detail, but I hadn't noticed it before. The people of Winslow sponsored this. Some are in memoriam.

"No shit, Woody," Dallas growls. And I get it. To pull her hands up she has to press herself to the back of the statue. It's an uncomfortable and exceedingly vulnerable position. "You remember our deal, right?" she asks.

She wants me to kill her before the Zs do. I ignore her and put all I've got on the ratchet and get it to tick tighter, once, twice, three times. The metal lever is pressing into my hands painfully, but I keep going.

The sound of the Zs is getting closer. I give myself five more seconds to do this and focus. Bearing down with my weight, grunting at the effort, sweating into my clothes. It moves again, four ticks more on the ratchet. It's not much, not much at all, but it's something.

The statue screeches forward very, very slowly, and I move with it.

"They are almost here," Dallas says, her head craning around awkwardly. "You need to take care of this. Now!"

She might mean getting the strap ratcheted up. She might mean me ending her life. I can think about it. I can feel the Zs, they are close. Their snarls suddenly loud as my ears start to recover from the blasts. I can smell their fetid fugal scent. I can almost feel them grasping for me.

My five seconds are up, but I give it one more hard shove and the ratchet ticks some more and the statue rises just a bit, the head being about an inch off the ground now.

I stand up, grab my bat, and shout, "Hit it!"

The Zs are on us, they are everywhere. It's not two hordes anymore, but one. The entire zombie population of Winslow, Arizona has converged on that corner, a sea of the mostly dead trying to feast on the only living things within reach.

Dallas is cursing and kicking at them as they grasp for her. I don't think. I can't think. There is no time and too much adrenaline. Even if I had had a gun, I wouldn't have used it. I hate guns. June has gotten me so I am trained and know how to use one, but even without Talia's rule I wouldn't have.

A bat, though, that is second nature to me, an extension of me. All those years playing baseball and I feel so comfortable with it in my hands.

I swing around me, breaking the arms of the Zs grasping for me, grasping for Dallas.

The engine of the Toyota revs and the statue screeches loudly as the truck starts to drag it along.

I step into the mass and keep swinging, clearing the grasping arms off of Dallas who is kicking with all her might at the Zs trying to get her.

I scream, I can't tell you what I said, maybe it wasn't even words, just the adrenaline and the desperation and the desire to survive.

I am way more like the Zs then. I am a creature of base need. The need to survive. That is all there is.

As the statue moves slowly forward with Dallas on top of it, I step into the space it vacated, use that distance and start swinging. More arms break, the snapping of the bone a sharp sound reminiscent of a bat hitting a speeding baseball. I smash skulls and for a moment it feels like I can do this. I can take them all on. I can survive.

I am lost to the moment. Lost to the battle.

"Woody!" Dallas screams.

And then awareness comes crashing down on me. The truck is twenty feet away and gaining momentum. The Zs have surrounded me and are closing in.

I met this guy named Park—that's his last name, I don't remember his first—on my way up to Flagstaff. I found him sitting on the pine-needle covered blacktop of I-17 just up the Mogollon Rim amongst the pine trees. He had flipped his car, he had broken his arm, and he was out of bullets.

He just sat there even though a group of zombies was about to descend on him. I screamed at him to get up and waded into the fight. I didn't understand why he was just sitting there. Sure, he didn't have much of a chance of living and it took me helping for him to survive, but I didn't believe there was ever a good enough reason to give up.

But there in Winslow on Route 66 on that famous corner, I finally understood Park. I understood that moment. I had the thought.

Wouldn't it be easier to just give up? Let the zombies take me, let the apocalypse win? Then all this struggle would be over. All this running. All this scraping for survival.

But unlike Park, I had a reason to live. Two reasons, two really good reasons. June and Dallas. Passionate love and deep friendship. The three of us had a bond forged out of the harshest of circumstances.

I notice little things, like the Zs' hands as they grasp for me. Flesh torn, pulled-back fingernails, broken fingers. The force that animated them past normal biology is not kind to them, it is using them more harshly than biology normally uses us.

I see their faces, past the ragged dirtiness of them, past the torn flesh and whites of their eyes gone yellowish. I see the former mothers and daughters, fathers and sons.

It is all just a moment, relating to Park's moment of giving up. Seeing the humanity that hasn't completely faded from the Zs. Remembering what I have to fight for.

And then I fight. I swing harder than I have ever swung in my life. I kick. I scream. I fight with everything I have, constantly moving, fighting towards the truck which I can still hear, the screeching quickly fading as it drags away the statue of Glenn Fry with Dallas handcuffed to it.

The bat and my fury keep them from completely overwhelming me, but I can feel them grasping at my back when I am swinging in the other direction. The stench of them is so strong it is a physical presence. I can taste it, moldy and fetid. It stings my nose. And the sound of their snapping jaws becomes louder than their snarls as they get closer to me, closer to their meal.

Even with how hard I am fighting, even with having so much to live for, the distance between me and freedom is getting thicker as the horde surrounds me.

It is not going to be enough. I am dimly aware of the drone buzzing closer to record my death. I am even more aware that I can't hear the screeching of the statue anymore.

I am alone and it is time to die.

My one comfort is that June and Dallas got away. That keeps a manic smile on my face as I keep fighting.

CHAPTER SEVEN

THE MARK of a good life is wanting more. Specifically, more of what you have. More time with the ones you love. More opportunities to say the important things.

And in that moment in Winslow, Arizona on the pavers that have a large painted Old Route 66 sign on them, I know I have had a good life. Despite the apocalypse, despite the horrors of Phoenix, despite Talia and all the challenges of surviving, despite all the loved ones that I have lost.

I have had a good life.

Because I want more. More time with June. More time with Dallas. I know that survival will be so hard, that it will never be easy, that we will never have the kind of safety and abundance as before the Zs, but I want more.

So I fight long past the moment when I had any chance of getting away from the zombie horde. I swing the bat and kick and grunt and sweat and push and struggle. My breath burning in my lungs still recovering from all the smoke in Two Guns, my stomach roiling at the stench of the zombies, my muscles screaming for rest.

They grasp my jacket and I twist around swinging my bat. Their fingernails scratch at my hands, drawing blood, but I ignore it. The struggle seems to last forever, the same sounds, the same moves, the same smells, until I hear something different.

I don't know what it is at first, a high-pitched sound but not like the drone. A rumbling sound. A happy sound. And then it hits me, I am hearing the sound of an engine revved to a high RPM.

And then I hear the wet sound of metal striking flesh and Zs are flying and I see our beautiful black truck plowing through the horde towards me. Bodies flying, the engine straining, the Zs fresh-brains radar locking onto another target and the press of them around me easing as their group mind decides what to do.

Suddenly there is hope and I fight with renewed strength. There's a wall five Zs thick between me and the truck which is now stopped. I swing like there is no tomorrow. I don't care about killing them, I only care about getting them out of the way.

Hands grasp my jacket, but I can't turn back now. I surge forward. I swing and swing. I clear my way to the truck and I see June.

She's in the driver's seat, her eyes on fire, her jaw set. She's screaming at me but I don't understand the words.

I just need half a step more and then I can jump on the hood, but I can't move, there are too many hands on my jacket. One of them grabs at my head and they tear off my beloved Diamondbacks base-ball hat.

The Zs are flowing in around the space that June opened up with the truck.

And then I can understand her. "Grab something!" she screams.

This is a new-when-the-apocalypse-happened truck, so the bumper, such as it is, is integrated into the front of the truck. There is only the grill to grab on to and it's not that strong. But I do. I drop my bat. I shuck off my jacket, and I grab onto the grill.

Our eyes meet briefly and I give her a small smile and nod. She shoves the truck into reverse and hits the gas, dragging me out of the grasping horde of zombies.

CHAPTER EIGHT

I LOST MY TALISMANS.

As June drags me out of the snarling, grasping, zombie horde, as I clutch the grill of the Toyota pickup truck, as I stumble along trying to keep up, as I kick at the Zs grasping for me and then end up being dragged along, it hits me.

I've lost my talismans and I feel naked and vulnerable without them. No, seriously.

My army surplus jacket with the seed packets I've carried since Phoenix. It represented the future and the life I wanted to live. A life of isolation where we can grow food and live in peace.

My Diamondbacks baseball hat that represented the past and my passion for baseball, both playing it and watching it. It connected me to my former life and my family and a time when this world made a lot more sense than it does now.

My baseball bat made out of hickory hewn from a tree that grew for decades, that was hard and resilient and had just saved my life... again.

I had lost baseball bats before, but the hat was from before the apocalypse and the jacket was from right after. It's like I don't know how to do this anymore without those things.

Once we're free of the Zs, the horde of them heading east down Route 66 after us, I stand up and shake out my hands. The plastic of the grill dug deeply into them.

There's two Zs that managed to hang on to the truck bed as June powered us out. I draw the knife from my belt and go to the one on the left. It comes for me, but I sidestep it, trip it, and hold its head down with one foot while I shove the thin knife through its eye.

By the time I stand up, June has gotten out of the truck and dealt with the other Z.

We have maybe thirty seconds before the horde gets to us.

"Dallas?" I ask.

June shrugs and nods down the road. "Still strapped to the statue down there."

We are on opposite sides of the truck just staring at each other. I'm shaking from adrenaline and exhaustion, from being so close to all those explosions, from losing my jacket and my hat, from coming so very close to dying and being zombie dinner.

"She must be pissed," I say.

June shrugs again and won't meet my eyes. She can be shy but I thought we were past that. Is she freaked out at how close I came to dying? Does she know what's coming next?

The sound of the Zs is getting louder and the damn drone just buzzed past us going east, down towards where Dallas must be.

"Thank you," I say. I mean it, I do, but there are more important things to say but I'm just too rattled to say them. Without my jacket, it's like I don't know that my plan of getting us to the White Mountains ever made sense, much less our decision to head back to the Grand Canyon. Without my hat, I feel exposed like the sky itself is dangerous.

"We better go," she says, nodding towards the Zs who are getting close.

I nod and get in the truck.

"WELL," Dallas yells when June stops the truck. "Did you rescue his skinny ass?"

She's handcuffed and chained to the statue of Glenn Frey in the middle of Route 66. June cut the tow rope and ratchet strap and just left her here to come rescue me.

We are out of the historic section of Winslow, which isn't that big. We're back into an industrial area with low, plain buildings with large garage doors to the north and open desert to the south between us and the train tracks. We're on a low bridge across a drainage area, some real green down there. The bridge makes the very vulnerable Dallas slightly less vulnerable.

We're not far from the corner, maybe a quarter mile. The Zs are still coming, the drone is hovering above us, and we are still in the middle of Talia's "game."

"Yeah," I say as I get out of the truck. "I'm alive. Escaped with nothing worse than a few scratches and a hole in my boot. You're not the only one that was dragged out of there by that truck. Disappointed I made it?"

I was underplaying it a little. Okay, a lot. I could feel the ghosts of several bites on my arms where the jacket had saved me, my legs were rubbery, and the scratches on my hands and forearms where the Zs were grasping for me with the ragged fingers were starting to burn, and more than just a few.

"Oh yeah," she says, twisting her head to look at me. "I was hoping to have June all to myself."

She looks ridiculous. Puffy pink jacket with the white faux fur trim lying on top of a bronze statue on the detritus-covered road.

"That so," I say, turning to June. "I think we should just leave her then."

It's not what June and I need to say, and maybe this just isn't the time for the conversation about how badly things almost went, but I still have the adrenaline flowing and I'm shaking and beat to shit from the day so far. I lost my Diamondbacks hat and my army surplus jacket and I feel exposed. Humor, poor humor, is the only shield I have left.

"That's a good idea," June says. There's a smile on her face, but not in her voice. "We'd have a lot more alone time that way."

"Hey!" Dallas yells. "Who finally got you two a room at the Grand Canyon? Who sat on the roof at that dirt-boat-thingy for hours and hours so you guys could have *alone* time over and over?"

"Earthship," I say, correcting her.

"Whatever," she shoots back. "I am the empowerer of your alone time. I'm the one that makes it safe for you two to be alone. You guys need me."

"Well..." I begin.

"I don't know," June says, sounding a little more cheerful. "She can be kinda useful, but she can also be kinda annoying."

"Annoying?" Dallas says, her voice pitching high. "I'm really the social lubricant that lets you awkward shy folks keep talking."

We are teasing Dallas because we need to let off steam. Because she teases us all the time. Because she is vulnerable. But she hit a nerve there and I can see it in the furrowing of June's brow. I love June, I love to spend time with her, but this is only day twenty-seven of Woody and June versus the Apocalypse. We do have these periods of awkwardness like we are having right now.

We are both silent, and Dallas swings her head back and forth trying to get a good look at us. "What? What the hell happened? Can someone get me the hell off this thing? I've decided that I am not desperate enough to settle for a statue. Besides, the guy keeps rubbing his hard back against me. It's creepy."

"I don't know how we're going to do that," I say.

"What?" Dallas asks, her voice pitching a little high.

"We don't have bolt cutters," I say, "and you and your boy-toy are lying on the chain and I can't get to it with a hacksaw. Besides, we don't have enough time to saw through a chain."

"Goddamnit, Woody!" she yells. "I will not fight Zs again

chained to a freaking statue. You're the gadget guy, just get me off of here!" She's got her feet planted and is trying to sit up, but with her hands cuffed around the neck of the statue she just looks like a stink bug rearing up to spray.

I sigh and nod to June. "Pull the truck around. We're going to have to drag her again. This is going to take longer than we have here."

"Woody!" she yells and then starts cursing at me with the kind of speed and fluency that only Dallas can manage.

June chuckles, it's pure schadenfreude, but at least there's a little bit of laughter today.

𝗑𝗑𝗑 𝗑𝗑 𝗑𝗑𝗑

WE DRAG her about another mile down Route 66, the bronze statue screeching and throwing sparks the whole way, and Dallas cursing loud enough for us to hear it over the screech.

This maneuver is actually necessary. By the time we got the statue ratcheted up again, the Winslow zombie horde was visible down the road.

At the edge of Winslow where the two parts of Route 66 run close is a narrow strip of grass with some trees. It's some kind of park. We drag Dallas in, stop close to a tree, cut the statue down and rig the tow rope so it's wrapped around the neck of the statue thrown over a thick tree branch that's about eight feet off the ground and hooked to the back of the truck.

We need to get the statue off the ground to cut her free.

She complains and curses the whole time, but it is what it is. We get the statue just off the ground with Dallas standing with her arms up high around the neck of the statue.

"What are we going to do?" she asks. I'm hacksawing the chain that runs from her cuffs down to the gap between the guitar and the statue's leg. The drone has left, it must be out of juice, but I'm sure they have an outpost somewhere around here and will be sending one back soon.

The sawing is going slow. It's a hacksaw versus a chain. It will work, but it will take time. And I hope we have enough time before the horde gets here.

June is pacing on the mostly dead grass not far away, watching for them. It's that kind of pacing. Quick steps, but not too far, snapping around and changing direction, our eyes never quite meeting when she looks this way.

She's watching for zombies, sure, but she's chewing over what has happened today. Well, it's still only morning, it's been a hell of a day so far.

I sigh. My body is less shaky, but I'm so tired, my muscles weak and aching, my lungs still straining from the smoke, my throat sore and my voice rough. I need to sleep for a couple of days and have some good meals and lots of water.

Not that any of that is going to happen.

"I'm going to saw through this chain and separate you from your boyfriend there," I say. "And then we are going to hacksaw the little chains between the cuffs so you are functional. And then we are all going to get in the truck and get the hell out of here."

"No," she says. "About this stupid-ass game of Talia's. It's only going to get worse from here."

I pause my sawing and look around the statue at Dallas. Her shoulder-length brown hair is a tangled mess, her face dirty, and her brown eyes wide. "What are we going to do?" she whispers.

And that has to be another part of June's distance and her pacing. Talia was someone she loved. Someone she has known much longer than me.

"We are going to survive, Dallas," I say, trying to put some punch in my voice, but it just comes out rough and tired.

She shakes her head and I get back to sawing. "It's going to get worse, Woody," she says.

And by worse she means one of us will die. That Talia will make these situations so bad until there is no way we can all survive. The "Standin' on the Corner" trap was supposed to be that for Dallas. She was not supposed to survive. If it wasn't for the dynamite, which Talia must have overlooked, she would have.

And I almost did.

"We'll survive," I say through gritted teeth as I saw faster.

CHAPTER NINE

WE ARE STILL in the park, the three of us sitting on the remnants of grass, Dallas finally free of the statue of Glenn Frey. She's a bit bruised up from her ride behind the truck and still has the cuffs on her hands and ankles because of the epoxied keyholes, but otherwise unharmed.

The horde is heading towards us, but we have just enough time for a bit of food. We are spaced evenly passing around a can of garbanzo beans, a stale granola bar, and a bottle of water. It's like we are an equilateral triangle, all of us the same distance away from each other, just close enough to pass the food.

We aren't right. Not individually, not collectively. If nothing else is working, this part of Talia's game is.

The food is helping and the shakes are receding, but I feel like I have the shakes emotionally. Like if I say something, they will hear it in my voice.

I told Dallas that we are going to survive, but after the race across the 40s, Two Guns and the Apache Death Cave, and then fighting zombies on the corner in Winslow, I don't know. I just don't know.

Talia is better organized than I imagined anyone could be in this world and did it so damn quickly. I had told June that I thought her new tribe would soon tire of her and all the energy she is putting into this. And they will, won't they? They have to, no matter how brutal she is, right?

But I just don't know.

It's silent except for the quiet sounds of chewing and the glug-glug of the water bottle.

It is too quiet. And then it hits me.

"The song," I say. It comes out as a croak and they both look at me, their brows furrowed. "The song," I repeat. "'Take it Easy'. When did it stop playing?"

Talia had been playing it over the walkie-talkie, a bizarre counterpoint to the decidedly not easy stuff we were doing.

June blinks and looks around. "Ummm..." she begins. "I... I think it stopped sometime when I was hauling Dallas off. But it was so noisy, I can't be sure." Her blue eyes connect with mine. "Why?"

"I don't know," I say, taking the can of garbanzos from Dallas.

"Woody..." Dallas says. "What is going through that crazy head of yours?"

I brush my hair out of my eyes. That's the other problem with losing my hat. My hair is too long, and I don't have the hat to contain it anymore.

I shrug. "Just makes me worried that Talia's up to something."

June gets up, grabs the binoculars from the hood of the truck. "The Zs are still coming," she says, "but we have time."

"No drone," I mumble as I get up and start scanning the sky. "That is weird."

"Maybe we should leave," Dallas says, standing up.

They are both staring at me. They want a plan. They want assurances that I have the slightest clue as to what might work. I'm the Arizona boy, this is my territory, so it falls to me. This after my plan to rest in the Earthship in the 40s and our night at Meteor Crater let Talia catch back up to us. Twice.

"East," I say, nodding down the road.

"Why?" June asks, folding her arms over her chest.

"Two reasons. The White Mountains are east and the 'direction' we got at Two Guns was east. It's the way we want to go and the way Talia wants us to go."

They are both just staring at me, and now that I hear it, it sounds like a bad idea to do anything Talia wants if we don't have to. I point to the west, "Our only other option is to get on the highway, try to circle around the horde, and go south from there."

"No," June says, the single syllable tight and clipped. The kind of "no" that is intended to cut off conversation. And I don't know if that's a "no" about heading east, about circling back, or about both.

"There must be something else," she says.

I run to the truck and grab the map and run back to our picnic site. While I know Arizona well, my memory is far from perfect. I spread the map out on the grass. There's a road heading north northeast not far to the east of us that goes up toward the reservation.

I point at it. "We can head up towards the rez. No idea what we will find, but..."

"Talia can't hold sway up there," June finishes.

"Well then," Dallas says, "let's get the hell out of here. Glenn Frey is starting to eye me and I'm not getting close to that dude again."

CHAPTER TEN

WHAT'S that old saying about plans? They don't survive the first contact with the enemy, that it's not about plans, it's about adaptability.

Talia had planned for Dallas to die on that corner in Winslow, but we all just managed to survive.

We planned to hightail it out of Winslow and head towards the north, but we paused, for twenty minutes, because we had to, and that gave Talia time to set other plans into motion. She is adapting to us just as we are adapting to her.

As we walk to the truck after our modest meal and brief rest, I feel a little lighter. My lungs hurt, my muscles are tired, and the array of scratches I got from the zombies burn, but I feel like I've got more in that tank now. That I can think just a little bit.

And then I hear a buzzing in the sky, like a nest of angry wasps. I look and see a drone heading towards us from the northeast, from where I-40 is.

I stop and stare. It doesn't look right. It's a ways away, but somehow looks misshapen and is moving sluggishly. My stomach tightens and I look all around, expecting danger to come from another direction, from several other directions.

The walkie-talkie crackles to life from the truck.

"Greetings survivors and players of my glorious game," Talia says, her voice positively cheerful, like she's well fed, well rested, and having the time of her life.

We all stop. I'm near the driver's side door, June near the passenger's with Dallas next to her.

"You've done well," she continues. "Better than expected, to be honest." And now there is some disappointment in her voice. "But... as I promised with the guns... you used dynamite so now we will use dynamite. And yes, I know I didn't explicitly prohibit the use of explosives, but the spirit of the rule was violated."

I turn back to the drone and it is closer and it's clear that it is carrying something, and it can only be one thing. Dynamite.

"You have until the drone reaches your truck to vacate the vicinity," she said. "The dynamite is rigged Woody-style, so I don't think you want to be anywhere near here."

"She's going to blow up the truck," I mumble. Not because anyone needs to hear it, but because I'm having trouble processing it. I lost my hat, my jacket, my bat, and now our truck?

And rigged "Woody-style" means there are nails glued to the dynamite making it a lot more deadly than what I used against the Zs on the corner.

"Bags!" June shouts, running towards the back door of the truck. It's survival 101, you *always* have a go-bag ready. In our case it's three stuffed backpacks. I run to the other side and open up the back door, shoulder my go-bag, and take about two seconds to toss other stuff out the door, hoping it might help with salvaging things later.

And then we are all running, back to the west, back toward the horde, because none of us want to run toward the dynamite-carrying drone.

There's no cover, only park and trees and road and desert. A couple of rusted pieces of metal standing tall. They look like the beams from a high-rise.

It hit me what this park is. A memorial to 9-11, those pieces of metal must be from the twin towers. We had stopped on the other end of the park and I hadn't noticed any of this.

Beyond the twin pieces of metal, the horde is just visible shambling towards us, no longer a tight grouping, the zombies having spread out a bit as their fresh flesh radar guides them in our direction.

"There!" June shouted, pointing at a worn chunk of cement that says, "Winslow, United We Stand." Probably concrete from the rubble that was left of the towers.

It is a strange feeling to remember that tragedy and the conflicts that raged around the world at that time. I was a kid when the towers came down, the image of it that they played over and over on TV haunted me at night for months. And here at this memorial to 9-11 that marks an old conflict, an old tragedy, we were playing out a new conflict, trying not to let it become a new tragedy.

Humans are still human, the zombies haven't changed that.

I glance back at the drone and it looks like we have just enough time.

June is out front, with Dallas right behind her and me bringing up the rear. We are running over the grass, avoiding the trees.

Yes, we have just enough time.

Dallas's ankle twists on her as her foot hits a soft spot in the ground and she goes down with a shout. I don't look back, I keep my momentum, grab her under her arm, yank her up, and drag her forward. She cries out, curses, and hobbles, and just as we are ducking behind the concrete a BOOM! shatters the silence and a wave of hot air rushes over us.

CHAPTER ELEVEN

WE FINALLY GET a Hollywood explosion out of the day.

The truck is toast. Total and complete. One hundred percent.

Not only was the tank nearly full of gas, we had about twenty gallons of gas in jerry cans in the back. And not only was there gas, there were about twenty sticks of dynamite in the truck.

We hear the boom. We feel the earth move under us. There is a wash of hot air and the sound of things striking the concrete we are hiding behind.

I lean against the cool, hard surface, my breath coming in ragged gasps and my heart thumping hard in my chest. In the distance, the Zs are still shambling towards, unmoved by what just happened.

"What the hell was that?" Dallas asks. She's on the ground, her jean leg pulled up as she looks at her swollen ankle. A zombie horde numbered in the thousands plus an injured ankle is a very bad thing.

June peaks around the corner and curses. I hear the sound of fire. I pause, staring at the distant Zs. I don't want to see what happened.

"At least it got the damn drone," June says.

Dallas snorts from her sitting position. "And the cursed walkie-talkie was in the truck, so now the queen bitch of the desert can't blab at us anymore."

They are handling this well. Looking on the bright side. But I'm still plastered against the cement breathing hard. A coughing fit takes me, my lungs still recovering from all the smoke this morning.

I'm dimly aware that I'm not quite right. I'm now staring at our go-bags and inventorying what we've got. Everyone has a knife, gun, and flashlight on their belt. All the go-bags have food, water bottles, basic hygiene stuff, and extra clothes.

My go-bag has gear, like little solar chargers, a battery-powered soldering iron, wire strippers, and miscellaneous electronics. It also has my journals. It feels like the writing of this is doing a lot to keep me sane.

June's is stuffed with ammo and first aid supplies.

Dallas has extra food, some maps, and a flask of whiskey.

There's something missing. My hands go to my head. No hat, my overlong hair getting in my eyes. My hand brushes the scab right at my hairline where Talia tried to blow my head off and would have but for June.

I don't have the weight of my jacket or my seed packets in the pocket. I lost those escaping the Zs on the corner.

And then it hits me. I don't have a bat. I lost that too. But there was one in the back of the truck. A crappy aluminum bat, but a bat nonetheless.

Before I know it, I have put my backpack on and am stumbling towards the truck, towards what's left of the truck.

It's on its side and burning as are all the trees close to it. The hood is gone and the driver's-side door is blown off, the frame twisted. It looks helpless and sad, like an animal that should be put down.

The ground around it is blackened and there is debris every-where. Pieces of metal. Burnt chunks of plastic. The half-burnt cover of Stephen King's *The Stand*.

We had been so well supplied, much of it inherited on the South Rim from a very well-supplied group that had come there but fallen to the zombie tourist horde.

And now all we have is what is on us and in our packs.

The smoke is acrid, not as thick as what we experienced in the Apache Death Caves, but caustic and dark. I am coughing and close enough to the burning truck to feel the heat, kicking through the remains.

I kick aside a good solar charger, a little bigger than my hand. I should pick it up, we could use it, but all I can think of is the bat. I need a bat. I've lost every possession that mattered to me, I won't leave without a bat.

"Woody?" June says gently, laying her hand on my arm. "What are you looking for, Woody?"

Dimly I am aware that she isn't treating me normally, that her voice is too gentle, her touch too tentative, but only dimly.

"We had an extra bat," I say, not looking at her. "I need a bat." I can't look at her, but I do see another set of feet. Well, one foot. She has Dallas and is helping her hobble along. I should do that. I am bigger. There are zombies coming, but I need a bat.

My bat saved me back there on the corner where a gun would have failed me. I swung hard enough and fast enough to keep them at bay.

I kick over a half-melted tub and ignore the canned goods that tumble out and stumble closer to the truck ignoring the heat, ignoring my coughing, and then I see it. It's sticking out from under a chunk of twisted metal, the hood of the truck.

I run over, a smile on my face like a kid spotting a gift and it's just what they wanted. I'm not right and part of me knows that. The heat from the burning truck is intense. My eyes are watering and I'm coughing hard, but I snag the bat, pull it from underneath the remnants of the hood. It's sleek aluminum and there is a small dent at the end, but it is a baseball bat. I am somehow okay now that I have a small part of my past back and a big part of my present identity.

Well, I think I'm okay, but I'm not. None of us are, but the obsession lifts and I see June helping Dallas hobble forward, to the east, away from the Zs. They are closer now and I can hear them over the crackling of the fire. We've got a few minutes lead on them, but that's not much with Dallas's ankle.

June glances my way and I see the look on her face, like she's afraid of me. Afraid of the man who was traipsing through the fire, ignoring the food in search of a bat. Like when she looks at me, she is reliving what happened less than an hour ago when she rescued me from the horde by driving the truck into them.

And that look sobers me up. Fast. Pulls me out of the strange mental fugue I was in. Brings me back.

Things don't matter. My bat doesn't matter. June and Dallas are what matters. Surviving is what matters. And to survive we need to leave. Now.

We passed plenty of abandoned cars on the way here, but that won't do us any good. There are some gas stations not far from here, but that's the direction the drone came from and Talia and/or her people are there.

We need something, anything, so we can keep moving.

And then I spot it. A bike. Just laying by the side of the road, nothing at all near it. Like someone just abandoned it. Which is how much of the world looks now.

I jog over and examine it. It's a faded blue single-speed bike with a big wicker basket on the handlebars, the graceful downward sweep of the center bar marking it as a "girl's" bike, not like that kind of thing matters anymore. It looks like it's from another time. But the wheels turn. The brakes work. I even ring the little bell on the handlebar.

I look back and the horde is spread out enough so it's on this side of Route 66, just passing a green sign that marks the city limits. "Entering Winslow. Elevation 4850. Founded 1880."

I stare at the sign for just a moment. There's something significant here, something important, but I just can't put it together. I shrug, put my bat in the basket, and jog the bike over to the slowly retreating June and Dallas.

June is looking at me, her ocean-blue eyes hard, searching, needing.

"I'm okay," I say. "I just had a moment."

And I am definitely more okay than I was, but not at all sure if I'm okay yet. And this is post-apocalyptic okay we are talking about here, not pre-. The metrics have changed dramatically. I doubt that she is okay either, and it's clear that we are not.

She holds my gaze for a few breaths and then she nods and we get Dallas on the bike, the snarling and shuffling of the horde getting louder.

We need the bike. Without it, with us helping Dallas to shuffle along, we are slower than the Zs. With it, we will be a little faster, and that's something.

After Dallas is perched on the bike, her good foot on a pedal, her hands gripping the handlebars, I get behind her and start pushing. I still have too much adrenaline and we need some breathing room.

June jogs easily beside me, her pack bouncing on her back, her blue eyes continuing to examine me. I notice that she has her rifle in her hand—she must have grabbed that with her go-bag.

"I'm... I'm going to be okay," I say.

Her brow furrows briefly and she smiles. It's a small thing, tiny really, but it gives me the hope I need to continue.

We may only have three go-bags, a few guns, one rifle, and a bike, but we have each other. So there is hope that we will get away from the Zs, get away from Talia, get somewhere we can rest, somewhere we can heal.

Dallas is bruised from her ride on Glenn Frey, has the purple going to yellow bruising on her face from Talia, handcuffs on her wrists and ankles with a link dangling from each, and has a badly sprained ankle—I hope it's just a sprain. Even if it is, we need to get the handcuff off there soon because of the swelling. June and I are still recovering from smoke inhalation, and those zombie scratches I got on my hands and forearms are burning like hell. Not to mention the gunshot wound to my arm or the scabbed-up wound on my forehead. June's face has recovering bruises courtesy of Talia too. And those are the wounds you can see.

And June and I need to talk through what happened today.

We are all a mess, but we are a "we." And we will find a way to survive.

I slow the jog down to a fast walk. We've got a little breathing room and I need to catch my breath. "Did you guys notice," I say, nodding back behind us. The significance of the Winslow city limit sign finally coming into focus.

"Notice what?" June asks, looking around like we've got another bomb-carrying drone on the way.

"Back there by the park is the 'Entering Winslow' sign."

"So?" Dallas asks from her perch.

"So... we survived Winslow," I say, and I sound happy. Maybe it's a little manic, but I'll take it.

They are both silent for a moment, June staring at me again.

"Well what do you know," Dallas says, breaking the silence. "Talia!" she yells into the blue sky. "You hear that, queen bitch of the desert?! We survived the town you rigged to kill us."

She takes one hand off the handlebar, raises her middle finger, and points it back towards Winslow. "I hope I never see Winslow again," she says, "and I hope I never hear that damn song again."

June is smiling, this time for real, and she walks over and kisses me on the cheek and whispers, "Thank you."

I'm not sure what this kiss or the thank you is for, but I'm glad for it and I smile for real, too. Dallas continues to shout her celebration of surviving Winslow as I push her down the road.

EPISODE 11
WOODY AND JUNE VERSUS THE INFECTION

More adventure, an unthinkable problem, and more Woody and June awaits you in.... *Woody and June versus the Infection*. Available 11/2022

To stay abreast of all things Woody and June, head over to WoodyAndJune.com and sign up for my e-mail newsletter and don't miss out on a thing! Plus, you'll get a free ebook that includes "Park's Law of the Apocalypse," a newsletter-exclusive story in the world of Woody and June.

🧟🧟🧟   🧟🧟   🧟🧟🧟

WOODY AND JUNE VERSUS THE INFECTION

Time for the Rescuer to be Rescued

Woody Beckman and June Medina defied the odds and found each other in post-zombie-apocalypse Arizona. No longer go-it-alone survivors, they now face the future together with something to lose. Each other.

When Woody, June, and Dallas survive the twisted trap Talia set for them in Winslow, Arizona things go from bad to worse when one of them comes face-to-face with Talia and then goes up against the deadliest foe yet, the zombie infection.

Can Woody and June beat the odds and let their love flourish in a world of zombies and psychotic, petty, wannabe warlords?

A story of adventure and love and taking things (even the apocalypse) in stride.

BEFORE YOU GO

Before you go, my book, *Bits, Bites, and Rarities: The Worlds of Robert J. McCarter* is a fantastic introduction to my series and worlds. It's only available to my newsletter subscribers, and the price is the best part. It's free!

This action-packed book contains 15 stories, is 750+ pages long, and has 4 exclusive stories that are not available anywhere else, including "Park's Law of the Apocalypse," a story in the world of Woody and June you can't read anywhere else.

Get it today at *RobertJMcCarter.com/newsletter*

ABOUT THE AUTHOR

Robert J. McCarter is the author of more than ten novels and over a hundred short stories. He is a regular contributor to *Pulphouse Fiction Magazine* and his short fiction has also appeared in *The Saturday Evening Post, Andromeda Spaceways Inflight Magazine, Everyday Fiction*, and numerous anthologies.

Robert writes in a variety of genres from contemporary fantasy to science fiction and just about everything in between. His diverse background–including a career in software engineering, growing up on a ranch riding horses, and acting–colors the stories he tells.

He lives in the mountains of Arizona with his amazing wife and his ridiculously adorable dogs.

Find out more at:
RobertJMcCarter.com

BOOKS BY ROBERT J. MCCARTER

WOODY AND JUNE VERSUS THE APOCALYPSE

For a great deal, pick up *Woody and June Versus the Apocalypse* a volume at at time!

Woody and June Versus the Apocalypse: Volume 1 (Episodes 1 - 7)

- Woody and June versus the Wannabe Warlord
- Woody and June versus the Fungus-Head Zombies
- Woody and June versus the Grand Canyon
- Woody and June versus the Ex
- Woody and June versus the Third Wheel
- Woody and June versus Phantom Company
- Woody and June versus the Daring Rescue

Woody and June Versus the Apocalypse: Volume 2 (Episodes 8 - 12) *Coming 2/2023*

- Woody and June versus the Chase (coming 9/2022)
- Woody and June versus Two Guns (coming 10/2022)
- Woody and June versus Winslow (coming 11/2022)
- Woody and June versus the Infection (coming 12/2022)
- Woody and June versus the Siege (coming 1/2023)

Find out more at WoodyAndJune.com

NEUTRINOMAN & LIGHTNINGIRL: A LOVE STORY

For a great deal, pick up *Neutrinoman & Lightningirl: A Love Story* a season at at time!

Season 1 (Omnibus edition of Episodes 1 - 3)

- Meteor Attack!
- Toxic Asset
- Protocol X

Season 2 (Omnibus edition of Episodes 4-6)

- Off Book
- Hard Times
- Elemental Factors

Find out the latest at Neutrinoman.com

For a complete list of books, go to RobertJMcCarter.com/books

www.ingramcontent.com/pod-product-compliance
Lightning Source LLC
Chambersburg PA
CBHW070647130626
46555CB00006B/2753